The BOY Who KNEW the LANGUAGE of the BIRDS

by MARGARET K. WETTERER ◆ illustrated by BETH WRIGHT

CAROLRHODA BOOKS

MINNEAPOLIS, MINNESOTA   USA

For Carl Edward Eason III, his father, and his grandfather—M.K.W.
I'd like to dedicate this book to my parents and grandparents—B.W.

LIBRARY OF CONGRESS CATALOGING-IN-PUBLICATION DATA

Wetterer, Margaret K.
    The boy who knew the language of the birds / by Margaret K.
Wetterer; illustrations by Beth Wright.
        p.   cm.
    Summary: Colum's ability to understand the language of the
birds gains him access as royal storyteller to the King's castle,
where he is accidentally changed into a dog and entrusted with
protecting the newborn prince from being kidnapped by fairies.
    ISBN 0-87614-652-3
    [1. Fairy tales.] I. Wright, Beth, ill. II. Title
PZ8.W54Bo   1991
[E]—dc20   90-39701
                                                        CIP
                                                         AC

Manufactured in the United States of America

1 2 3 4 5 6 7 8 9 10 00 99 98 97 96 95 94 93 92 91

Once upon a time in the west of Ireland, in the ancient kingdom of Connaught, there lived a boy named Colum who understood the language of the birds. He had learned it as a child note by note, just as naturally as he had learned the language of humans word by word.

When Colum was still very young, his mother recognized her son's strange talent. "Tell no one about it," she warned. "It brings bad luck to speak of magic things." So the boy grew and learned and never told anyone his secret.

Colum's greatest pleasure was listening to birds talking to one another. Flocks of geese back from their summer in Iceland, darting swifts from Africa, swans from distant Russia—all the far-flying birds had tales of strange lands and exotic people.

Everything he heard from the birds Colum repeated to his mother and father, and later he told the stories to his friends. By the time he was nine years old, people throughout Connaught knew him for his marvelous tales. Often they asked him where he learned his stories, but Colum remembered his mother's warning, and he kept his secret.

In time, news of Colum's storytelling reached the king of Connaught. "I shall call the lad to the castle," said the king, "and he will tell us these wondrous tales."

Colum was delighted by the summons. How exciting it would be to meet the king, to see his mighty warriors, to walk within the castle grounds.

He waved goodbye to his mother and father, and, sitting on a big horse behind the king's messenger, he rode down the long road to the castle.

When he arrived, servants showed him to the great hall to meet the royal family. The king and queen were handsome and elegant, and their daughter, Princess Donella, was beautiful beyond anything Colum had ever imagined. What an honor it would be to serve such splendid people, he thought.

The royal family treated Colum with the greatest courtesy. If they were disappointed in his plain looks or his homely manners, they did not show it in any way. "Welcome, Colum," said the king. "We have heard you are a gifted storyteller. We delight in good stories and hope your tales will help us to forget our cares."

At these words Colum became aware of an air of sadness about the king and his family. With their power and riches, with their handsome looks and loyal followers, didn't they have everything one could wish for in this world?

From the servants, Colum soon learned the sad truth. A few years after Princess Donella was born, the queen had given birth to a son, but when the child was only a few days old he mysteriously disappeared. Then two years later, despite all precautions, another newborn prince vanished the same way. Everyone believed that fairies stole the boys, but all attempts to contact the Fairy World and recover the royal sons failed.

In those days, signs of magic and the Fairy

World were everywhere. Enchanted trees and wells were not at all unusual, and throughout Ireland there were many strange mounds that people called fairy forts. One stood not far from Colum's own cottage. It was a circular, grass-covered structure, about twice the size of a farmhouse. Colum and his neighbors believed that fairies dwelt within the fort, and they avoided it as a place of magic and danger.

But surely, thought Colum, the king's family should be safe inside the great stone walls of the castle. Fairy forts and fairy magic seemed shut out and far away. And yet, somehow, someone or something had spirited away the king's two sons.

Every evening after supper, Colum told a story for the king and his family. He told tales he had heard from gray owls about rival teams of cluricauns who played hurly in the meadows on moonlit nights. He described the underwater castle of the merman king and the frolics of his mermaid daughters exactly as he had heard from the sea birds. He told stories of wonder and mystery he'd overheard from birds that had journeyed to Ireland from distant parts of the world. And if it seemed to him that the Princess Donella particularly enjoyed a certain story, he tried to tell another like it.

"Where did you learn these wonderful stories?" the king asked Colum one evening.

Colum remembered his mother's warning and answered, "Sire, they come to me," which was true enough, but revealed nothing.

One day the king made an announcement. "The queen is soon to give birth to another child. Haul up the drawbridge. Bolt shut the castle gates. No one may enter or leave the castle grounds."

Only the birds, who flew over the high stone walls, who nestled in the battlements and sang at the castle windows, were free to come and go unchallenged.

Soon the day came when the queen's baby was born. It was a handsome boy, and, like his two brothers before him, he had his father's dark hair and his mother's violet eyes.

The king and queen were happy at the birth of their son, but fearful for his safety. The new prince must not be stolen the way his brothers had been. The king placed guards around the infant's cradle. He ordered the blacksmith to secure the nursery window with iron bands and bolt the nursery door with a great iron lock. The king knew that creatures from the Fairy World cannot pass through iron bars.

Day after day for a whole week, everyone in the castle was on the lookout to protect the new prince from fairy treachery. No one, except Colum, had any time at all for the Princess Donella. She felt ignored and neglected. She wandered listlessly around the castle grounds. My mother and father think only of the new baby now, thought the princess. Even the fairies steal only boys. Nobody cares about me.

It grieved Colum to see the beautiful princess so sad. He longed to see her smile, to hear her laugh. He tried in every way he could to cheer her, but his stories no longer interested the princess.

"I wish there were someone or something to amuse me," grumbled the princess.

Just then Colum heard two thrushes singing in a hazel tree that grew in the courtyard.

"Listen to that foolish princess," piped one bird to the other. "Little does she know that she could have her wish."

"Indeed, she could have three wishes," the other bird chimed in, "if she had the magic branch on which we sit."

Colum was overjoyed. Yes, he thought, that would surely amuse her. He reached up and snapped the branch from the hazel tree, and the birds flew off.

"Here, my princess," he said, stripping the leaves from the branch. "This is a magic stick. You can make three wishes."

Princess Donella stared at him in surprise. "What a silly thing to say," exclaimed the princess. "That is an ordinary branch. I saw you break it from the tree."

"It is not an ordinary branch. Please make a wish," urged Colum.

In reply, Princess Donella just laughed at him.

"You can make three wishes," Colum insisted. "This is a magic stick. The birds say so."

"Storyteller," declared the princess, "no one knows the language of the birds."

In his eagerness to please the princess, Colum completely forgot his mother's warning. "I know their language," he protested. "I understand everything the birds say."

"Then tell me, what did they say to make you think this stick is magic?" asked the princess.

"They said that you could have three wishes if you had the magic branch on which they sat. This is the branch. Please, take it and make a wish."

"Storyteller, I think you believe your own stories," Princess Donella declared as she took the branch Colum eagerly held out to her. "A magic stick, indeed!" she said bitterly. "It's like something you would throw to a dog." She thought for a minute, then laughed again. "That's it. I'll throw the stick, and you can fetch it," she said. "I wish you were a dog."

There was a flash of light and a loud cry that ended in a whine, and Colum, the boy, was gone. In his place stood a large shaggy hound.

Princess Donella dropped the magic stick in horror. Amazed and frightened by what had happened, she turned and ran away from the big dog, who stood staring after her in surprise. How can I explain this to my mother and father? was her first thought. What will I say when they ask for their storyteller? She stopped. Of course. I must wish that horrible dog back to a boy at once, she decided. And then, then I will have the third wish for myself. She returned to look for Colum, but he had gone and taken the magic stick with him. He will come back to me sooner or later, she thought. She strolled to her room, dreaming of the wonderful things she might wish for once she had the magic stick.

At first Colum was horrified to find himself changed into a dog. Princess Donella made a terrible wish, he thought, but she did not really mean to do this to me. He ran off with the magic stick, planning to wish himself back to a boy again as soon as he was out of sight of everyone.

As he ran through the courtyard, past the kitchen garden, and along the castle wall, Colum began to be aware of exciting new sensations. He sniffed scents he had never smelled before—the smell of hatred from a cat that watched him from the kitchen steps, the smell of fear from a rabbit hiding in the shrubs. His nose twitched to far-off smells of deer and wolves and wild things.

Colum heard sounds he had never noticed before. His hound's ears picked up growls and grunts, yelps and cries, calls and murmurs of people and animals.

Colum gazed about him through new eyes, and in his heart he laughed at the thought of this grand adventure. I will remain a dog for just a

little while, Colum thought. It will be fun to see what it is like to be a dog. So he buried the magic stick in the corner of the yard.

Colum raced around the castle grounds testing his powerful legs. He jumped, rolled, and leapt in the joy of newfound strength and abilities. Warriors and maids and workmen smiled when they saw the familiar-looking dog frolicking. He seemed to be expressing their own happy mood. A whole week had passed, and the new prince was still safe and snug in his nursery.

At last Colum lay down by the kitchen door. He felt hungrier than he ever had before, and he hoped the kitchen maid might give him something to eat. When the young maid saw the huge dog outside the kitchen door, she was startled. But because he looked so familiar and had such friendly eyes, she soon returned with a bowl of food.

It was a beautiful, sunny afternoon, and the king and queen decided that since one whole week had safely passed, it would be all right to take their son for a walk in the castle courtyard.

Colum was finishing his bowl of food when he heard sparrows chirping in the rosebush that grew around the kitchen door. "The Fairy Queen has sent a henchman in the form of an eagle. It is watching and waiting to snatch the prince away."

"An eagle, indeed! Why doesn't she steal him the way she did the others?"

Colum didn't wait to hear more. He bounded into the courtyard just as an eagle swooped and snatched the baby in its great talons. Colum leaped high in the air and caught the eagle's wing in his teeth. The bird released its claw hold, and the baby dropped back into his mother's out-stretched arms. The eagle succeeded in breaking loose, but it left behind a clutch of feathers in Colum's jaws. The bird flew off before the king's sword or the warriors' arrows could touch it.

The queen clasped her infant to her bosom and rushed indoors, followed by the weeping nursemaid and servants.

The king looked at the great hound sitting on its haunches before him. "I have seen this dog before. Who owns it?" he asked. No one knew. "I want this dog to guard the prince. He saved my son when no one else could."

The king himself led Colum to the nursery to guard the baby.

When Princess Donella heard the story of the dog who rescued the prince, she knew at once that it was Colum. She went to the nursery and found him lying beside the baby's cradle.

"I am glad you saved my brother," she said politely. Then she added in a coaxing whisper, "Give me the magic stick. I will wish you back to a boy again. Soon my mother and father will ask for their storyteller, and I will have to explain what happened to you. Why are you waiting? Let me make the wish now."

"Please, not yet," answered Colum, for he had not lost the power of human speech. "As a dog I can watch the prince closely. Perhaps I can protect him from the fairies."

"Do give me the magic stick," Princess Donella urged. "I will wish that my brother not be taken."

Colum was sorely tempted to do as the beautiful princess desired.

"But what of your other brothers?" Colum asked. "They may be with the fairies, but they have not yet been gone seven years. There is still time to save them. Perhaps I can learn of their whereabouts. Later I can wish myself back to a boy, and there will still be one wish left on the stick for you."

At twilight, as Colum lay beside the prince's cradle, he heard two crows cawing in the tree outside. Their voices were so loud he could hear them even through the shuttered window.

"Tonight the Fairy Queen will steal the baby," cawed one crow.

"So I've heard," replied the other. "But how?"

"The same way she stole his brothers," was the answer.

"Oh. Then anyone who drinks water from the castle well or eats food that is cooked in it will sleep soundly tonight," chuckled the second crow, and both flew off.

That evening Colum neither ate nor drank anything, although the kitchen maid tried her best to coax him.

The guards took their places outside and inside the nursery door. A young servant boy fixed a fire against the chill of the evening and took his place in a chair beside the fireplace to watch it. The nursemaid rocked the baby to sleep, then took her place in the cot nearby. And Colum lay down beside the young prince's cradle.

By eleven o'clock the guards, the servant boy, the nursemaid, and all the living things in the castle were sound asleep. Even the fire slowly died down and went out. Only Colum remained awake and alert.

An hour passed and nothing happened.

Then, as the great yellow moon was rising over the treetops, a large red hand and arm swooped down the chimney and out of the fireplace and snatched the baby from the cradle.

Colum leaped up and sank his teeth into the red wrist. Blood spurted over the cradle, and the red hand released the child. Colum held on to the wrist, shaking it and twisting it while the arm steadily dragged him across the floor toward the fireplace. Then a second red hand swept down the chimney and snatched the baby away.

Colum released his hold on the first hand to catch the second one, but he was too late. Both hands and the baby were gone.

At that moment the guards awoke. The servant yawned and stretched, and the nursemaid rubbed sleep from her eyes. Then they saw the empty cradle, and Colum's muzzle covered with blood.

"The prince is gone," shouted the guards.

"The prince is gone," echoed the servant boy.

"The hound has killed the prince," cried the nursemaid, and she opened the nursery door to run and wake the queen.

Colum sprang through the door with the guards after him. He bounded out of the castle, ran to the corner of the yard and dug up the magic stick. As the guards had their swords raised to kill him, Colum cried, "I wish I were outside the castle."

Afterward, some of the guards claimed they saw the dog jump over the castle walls; others thought he had leapt right through the solid stones. All agreed they had heard him speak.

"They heard the dog speak! It was a pooka, an evil fairy animal. And I brought him into the castle myself," moaned the king.

Princess Donella alone could guess what had happened. He has used the second wish, she thought. Now there is only one wish left.

When Colum found himself safe outside the castle walls on the other side of the moat, he thought for a moment that he would go back and tell the king what had happened. Then he heard the sound of the drawbridge being lowered. He heard the shouts of the warriors in pursuit. If they caught him as either a dog or a boy, they might kill him before he could explain. Quickly Colum fled down the road toward home. He was going back to his mother and father. He could run faster as a dog. As soon as he got close to home, he would wish himself a boy again. He would never go back to the castle.

All through the long night he ran. A cock crowed. Creatures of the day stirred. Birds exchanged greetings and gossip. Colum paid little attention to them as he ran on. His mind was fixed on home. He was almost there. Then he heard corncrakes in a field, cackling and gossiping while they searched for worms. "The Fairy Queen is having a celebration tonight at the fort," said one.

Colum slowed down to listen.

"She has a third human child," another bird cawed.

Without thinking, Colum hastened toward the corncrakes to hear more, but he frightened them, and they rose in a flutter and flew off.

A third human child? That must be the king's son. That was the child the king had trusted him to guard from harm, and he had failed.

Colum stopped. He thought of the king and queen now sorrowing for their lost child. If only Colum could rescue all the king's sons from the fairies. Such a heroic deed would surely prove he was worthy of their trust, and worthy, too, of Princess Donella's respect and perhaps even her admiration.

Now Colum was before his own house. He hesitated; he looked at it longingly. Then he passed it by and ran instead into a wooded grove near the fairy fort.

Yes, he would try to rescue the king's sons. He would remain a dog for one more day. If he were a boy, fairies would hide their comings and goings from him. They would pay little attention to a dog. Succeed or fail, tomorrow he would use the last wish and become a boy again.

The day passed slowly while Colum hid and waited for the dark.

That night as the moon rose, Colum lay close by the fairy fort with the magic stick in his mouth. After a time he heard a rush of wind and saw leaves and straw swirl in the air. The wind died, and the leaves became full-size coaches, and the straw became magnificent horses. Beautiful fairy women stepped from the coaches, and handsome fairy men dismounted from the horses.

"Open, open!" they cried. "Open for the invited."

A stone rolled back, and the side of the fairy fort opened, and the fairies entered.

Colum glimpsed bright light and heard the strains of lively music before the opening in the fort slammed shut again.

He drew nearer.

Soon he heard the wind rushing, and again he saw leaves and straw whirl in the air. As before, they turned into coaches and horses, and fairy men and women appeared.

"Open, open! Open for the invited," they cried. Colum crept closer, and when the fairies entered, he sprang in behind them before the rock rolled back.

Colum caught his breath in amazement. On the outside, the fort was no more than forty feet across. Yet inside, he looked upon a scene that stretched on and on to a distant horizon. Outside the fort, he knew, the moon was rising in the night sky, but here it seemed to be noon of a

bright sunny day. In a lovely green meadow, beneath a striped canopy, a beautiful woman rocked a baby in a golden cradle. Nearby, two handsome dark-haired boys played with a golden ball. The king's three sons, Colum thought. Seated on a stone wall, a fiddler played a haunting tune, and many fairy men and women joined hands in a graceful dance. Three giants stood beside a tree, talking. One of them had his arm in a sling. Could it be he who had snatched the baby from the cradle?

No one paid any attention to Colum, and he could see why. There were pookas everywhere—fairy horses, rabbits, goats, cats, and dogs.

Colum noted carefully the rock that marked the entrance to the fort. He hoped the same words the fairies had used to get in would open the way out for him. Then he moved toward the children, slowly, slowly so as not to attract attention. As he passed groups of laughing, rollicking fairies, some offered him food and drink in fine gold and silver bowls, but he just nodded and passed on.

He was close enough to the children to see the violet color of their eyes when the Fairy Queen arose and lifted her hand.

Silence fell over the fairy throng.

The Fairy Queen looked at Colum, and his heart pounded and the hair on his back bristled. Then her glance drifted away over the crowd, and she spoke.

"Tonight I go to the Eastern Kingdom. Tonight I deliver these three human children, king's sons, to the Fairy King of the East. In exchange, I will rule the Western Kingdom unchallenged. My power will grow, and yours will grow, too. This is a time to celebrate. The war with the King of the East is over."

The fairies rose to their feet shouting and cheering. The fiddler struck up a wild tune, and the dancers stepped and whirled to the music. The Fairy Queen laughed and ran to join the dance. Other fairies hurried to the ring, too. Now everyone was dancing to the stirring music.

Colum padded up to the children, put down the magic stick, and lay beside the cradle. "Come, boys," he invited, "climb upon my back for a ride. You can hold the baby in your arms," he said to the older boy.

For a moment the children looked at the great friendly hound. Then the older boy lifted the baby from the cradle, and the brothers climbed onto Colum's back.

Colum picked up the magic stick in his mouth and as swiftly as he could, he ran with the boys toward the rock where he had entered the fairy fort. He was almost there; he was about to call, "Open," when someone noticed them.

"Look! Look! That hound is taking the king's sons."

"Stop him. Stop him." The cry rang everywhere.

Fairies closed in upon him from all sides. Before him stood the Fairy Queen, her arms flung wide, her face contorted with anger. There was no escape.

"I wish we were back in the castle," cried Colum.

There was a flash of light and angry screams, and as the noise died away, Colum found himself with the king's sons inside the empty castle nursery.

The older child lifted the baby into the cradle, and Colum wearily lay down on the floor beside it. The exhausted boys nestled their heads against Colum's heaving, furry sides, and all fell asleep.

In the morning the nursemaid thought she heard a baby's cry and went to the nursery to investigate. What joy there was in the castle when the king and queen learned that not just their baby, but their other two sons were home again. They had been stolen back from the Fairy World, and therefore the fairies could never take them again.

"Now," said Princess Donella to Colum when at last they were alone. "Now you must give me the magic stick, and I will wish you back to human form."

"It is too late," replied Colum sadly. "I used the last wish to escape with your brothers from the fairy fort. I must remain a dog forever."

"Oh, that is truly a terrible thing," said the princess. "But don't worry. I will tell the servants to see to it that you are well fed and cared for. It will be unpleasant for me to explain to my father how his storyteller became a dog, but I'm sure he won't be too displeased with me because he is so happy that you rescued my brothers." And the beautiful Princess Donella hurried away to join them.

While the castle rang with the joyous celebration over the return of the king's three sons, Colum fled unnoticed down the long road to his parents' little cottage.

It was dark when he reached home. His heart was so heavy that he could not go in. All night he lay in the shadows outside the door. The moon had set and the stars had faded in the pale light before dawn when Colum saw a stately woman walk up the path toward him. It was not until she stood looking down at him that he recognized the Fairy Queen.

"You stole the king's sons from me, and with your magic you ruined my plans," she said. "But you will pay dearly for your interference. Never again will you have any magic about you. Never any magic. No magic at all!" She waved her hand above Colum, and a wisp of heather fell upon him.

Colum's ears rang, and he shut his eyes against the sudden flare of burning light.

When he opened his eyes again, the sun had risen and the Fairy Queen was gone.

Colum looked at his hands and his feet. He was a boy again. The magic spell was gone with the fairy's curse.

Barnyard birds were cackling and calling excitedly. Nearby a curlew trilled and burbled as she rose in the morning sky. Colum listened. What were the birds saying? He strained his ears to hear. He could make out the notes clearly, but he could not understand them.

So this was the full meaning of the Fairy Queen's curse.

Just then his mother opened the door and threw her arms around him. "Colum, Colum, my son, you have come home. Father, Father! Our darling boy is home."

Colum never again returned to the castle nor saw the beautiful Princess Donella. But he never forgot all the stories he had heard from the birds, and when he grew up, he traveled all over Ireland collecting more stories. Everywhere he went, nobles and commoners welcomed him and honored him for the wonderful tales he told.

Never again, though, did Colum understand the language of the birds.